Queen
of the Universe

Written by Libby Gleeson
Illustrated by David Cox

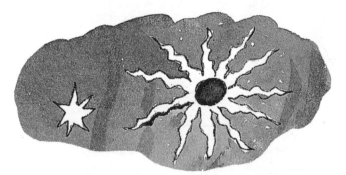

An easy-to-read SOLO
for beginning readers

Scholastic Canada Ltd.
New York Toronto London Auckland Sydney
Mexico City New Delhi Hong Kong

Scholastic Canada Ltd.
175 Hillmount Road, Markham, Ontario, Canada L6C 1Z7
Scholastic Inc.
555 Broadway, New York, NY 10012, USA
Scholastic Australia Pty Limited
PO Box 579, Gosford, NSW 2250, Australia
Scholastic New Zealand Limited
Private Bag 94407, Greenmount, Auckland, New Zealand
Scholastic Ltd.
Villiers House, Clarendon Avenue, Leamington Spa,
Warwickshire CV32 5PR, UK

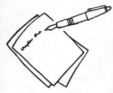

First published by Omnibus Books, part of the
SCHOLASTIC GROUP, Sydney, Australia.

National Library of Canada Cataloguing in Publication Data
Gleeson, Libby
    Queen of the universe
(Solo reading)
ISBN 0-439-98879-9
I. Cox, David, 1933- II. Title. III. Series.
PZ7.G557Qu 2001   j823   2001-900545-8

5 4 3 2 1   Printed and bound in Canada.   1 2 3 4 / 0

For Jo and Jess, the actors in my family – L.G.

For Bridie – D.C.

Chapter 1

"I'm in the school play," said Gina, at dinner time.

She's four years older than me.

"That's nice," said Mum.
"Good for you," said Dad.

"I'm not in it," I said. But nobody heard.

"Squeak, squeak," said Mouse.
He's my little brother, and he's
only three. This week he's Mouse.
Last week he was Dog.

"I'm the star," said Gina. "Ms. Hill made me the Queen of the Universe. I send my spaceships to the moon and the stars and the planets."

"I want to be a spaceman,"
I said. But nobody heard.

Mum looked at Gina. "OK,
Queen of the Universe, it's your
turn to clear the table."

Chapter 2

"I want to be in the school play too," I said to Mum. We were washing up.

"You're too young," she said.
"You can help me make Gina's
costume."

"I want to be in the school play too," I said to Dad. He was reading me a story.

9

"You're too young," he said.
"You can help me make Gina's
spaceship."

"I want to be in the school play too," I said to Gina, after the lights went out.

"You're too young," she said.
"You can help me learn my lines."
"I don't want to be too young,"
I said. "I don't want to help
anyone."

But I did.

Chapter 3

Mum got shiny silver paper and
I helped cut out a crown for the
Queen of the Universe.

Duck watched and said,
"Quack, quack."

Dad got bits of wood and I helped hammer and nail a spaceship for the Queen of the Universe.

Cat watched and said, "Meow,
meow."

Gina and I sat on the bedroom floor and she said her words for the play.

I listened.

I listened at breakfast.

I listened on the way to school.

I listened on the way home.

Soon I knew Gina's lines as well as she did.

Chapter 4

Every day, at lunchtime, I went to the hall.

Ms. Hill walked up and down.

"No. No. *No*," she yelled at the
spacemen and their space dogs.
"That is not the way to come on
stage. Come from the other side."

She grinned at my sister. "Yes,
Gina. You come on now. No, Ann.
Come to the front of the stage."

Ms. Hill got red in the face and put her hands over her eyes. "*Why am I doing this?*" she said.

A week before the show, a
spaceman tripped over his space
boots. He fell into the curtain at
the back of the stage. The curtain
dropped on everyone.

Ms. Hill put her hands over her eyes. "Why am I doing this?" she said.

Three days before the show, a
space dog called Snickers
(because it's chocolate all over)
jumped off the stage and got its
leg stuck in a can of red paint. It
ran around and howled. It looked
like raspberry ripple ice cream.

The whole school came running.

Ms. Hill put her hands over
her eyes. "Why am I *doing* this?"
she said.

Chapter 5

The day before the show, Gina woke up with spots on her face.

"Chicken pox," said Mum.

"Chicken pox," said Dad.

"Cheep, cheep," said Bird.

"I can't have chicken pox,"
cried Gina. "I'm the star." She put
Mum's makeup on over the spots.

"Wash your face and go to bed,"
said Mum. "No show for you."

Chapter 6

I took a note for Ms. Hill. I waited
for her to put her hands over her
eyes and say, *"Why am I doing this?"*

She didn't.

She bit her lip. "The show must go on," she said. She sat down next to me.

"Have you been helping Gina learn her lines?"

"Yes."

"Do you know them all?"

"Yes."

"Can you say every word right now?"

"Ye–es." I knew what she wanted.

"No," I said. "No way. Not the Queen of the Universe. I'll be a spaceman, a space driver or a space dog. I'm too young. I'm too little."

"You will be the Queen of the Universe," said Ms. Hill, "and you will do it well."

She grabbed my arm and dragged me to the hall.

She got Gina's costume and
stuck pins in it everywhere.

She got a fluffy mop from the
storeroom and dropped it on my
head.

She got boxes to put inside the spaceship to make me taller.

And all the time she made me
say the lines, and I knew every one.

Chapter 7

So I did it.

Gina was in bed, all spotty, and I was on stage.

I wore her crown and I stood on a box to make me bigger and I said every line.

I sent my spaceships to the moon
and the stars and the planets.

I was the Queen of the Universe, and at the end of the play everyone clapped and cheered and stamped their feet.

Ms. Hill clapped the loudest.
She told everyone that Gina was
sick. "But," she said, "her brother
has saved the play."

Mum and Dad waved from the front row.

Everyone came backstage.

"Well done, son," said Dad.
"Great," said Mum.
"Croak," said Frog.

Libby Gleeson

I grew up in a family of six children and now I have three girls of my own. When I was little I told stories all the time. Now I write them down. There are always lots of stories in families.

Queen of the Universe began when I was thinking about the way little kids often follow older brothers and sisters around, admiring them, even though they seem to fight and argue all the time.

David Cox

I love drawing, and what I like most is to draw people in all kinds of moods and poses. When I am drawing someone who is angry, I make myself feel angry, or, if the person is happy, I smile and smile. In *Queen of the Universe* there are lots of different moods and lots of different movements. I had a good time doing these drawings.